FROM THE EARTH TO BEYOND THE SKY

FROM THE EARTH TO BEYOND THE SKY

Native American Medicine

EVELYN WOLFSON

Illustrated by Jennifer Hewitson

Houghton Mifflin Company
Boston 1993

Acknowledgments

My sincere thanks to all the people who helped with this book,
especially my sister Dorothy Tweer, husband Bill Wolfson,
and friends, Betty Lowry, Charlotte DeVoe, Helga Volkema, and
Bennett Simon.

I am especially grateful to Professor Elisabeth Tooker
of Temple University for reading and critiquing the entire
manuscript.

Library of Congress Cataloging-in-Publication Data

Wolfson, Evelyn.
  From the earth to beyond the sky : Native American medicine / by
Evelyn Wolfson ; illustrated by Jennifer Hewitson.
    p.   cm.
Includes bibliographical references and index.
  ISBN 0-395-55009-2
  1. Indians of North America—Medicine. 2. Shamanism—North
America. 3. Indians of North America—Ethnobotany. 4. Indians of
North America—Religion and mythology.   I. Hewitson, Jennifer.
II. Title.   92-46035
E98.M4W65   1993   CIP
610'.8997—dc20   AC

Printed in the United States of America
BP   10 9 8 7 6 5 4 3 2 1

To my daughter, Dacia,
with much love, admiration,
and appreciation

Contents

"Teach your children what we have taught our children, that the Earth is our mother . . . The air is precious to the red man, for all things share the same breathing — the beast, the tree, the man, they all share the same breath."

> — Chief Seattle, at the tribal assembly of 1854,
> prior to signing the Indian Treaties

Preface

Native Americans lived close to nature and understood both pain and pleasure. They were almost disease-free before the arrival of European missionaries, explorers, trappers, and settlers and had a firm understanding of the science of illness. Their medical practices were as good as and often better than those of their European counterparts. They developed a keen knowledge of anatomy from carving up animal carcasses and became expert at setting broken and dislocated bones, using splints made out of strips of bark which were molded to fit injured joints.

Native Americans also practiced personal hygiene and sophisticated childbirth methods, understood the cosmetic and antiseptic value of plant juices and oils, induced and prevented diarrhea, tied off arteries to prevent blood loss, pulled teeth, used pain killers, and practiced advanced forms of psychotherapy. They stored herbs at home and used them to cure common ailments. When these home remedies did not work, they went to tribal healers who had a greater knowledge of plant medicines and supernatural powers. Tribal healers dealt with gout, boils, tumors, abscesses, diabetes, dropsy, epilepsy, rheumatism, arthritis, urinary problems, burns, and frostbite — many of the same illnesses treated by medical specialists today.

Native Americans believed illness to be caused by angry spirits, and the job of curing was considered well done only after the spirits had been properly consulted and thanked. Native Americans held great celebrations to honor their spirits, and many included healing rituals.

Few tribes dealt with spirits, the supernatural, and healing in the same way. Spiritual practices differed from tribe to tribe because there was no single Native American religion. Each tribe's spiritual life was shaped by its environment.

Plains tribes, who depended on the buffalo to meet all their needs held elaborate celebrations to honor the animal they hunted. Tribes of the Northeast, who relied as much on agriculture as they did on hunting, held celebrations each year, thanking spirits on this earth and above. Pueblo tribes, who depended almost entirely on crops, held summer and winter solstice celebrations honoring weather spirits; and the Navajo, who were neither farmers nor hunters but sheepherders, conducted ceremonies to maintain harmony in the universe. Large tribal ceremonies often included healing rituals.

Native Americans had no word for medicine as we know it today. To them, medicine involved a whole array of ideas and sensations, not just remedies. Good medicine came from beautiful mountains, clean bodies of water, and clear rays of sunshine. It burst forth from a continuing cycle of birth, death, and renewal. Everything in the universe was connected and dependent on something else. Today Native American medicine is often symbolized by large, round medicine wheels or sacred circles.

The European settlers brought with them medicinal plants of their own but relied on Native Americans to teach them about new plants and cures. Many drugs that are commonly used today had been used by Native Americans for hundreds of years. Salicin, a substance found in most species of willow shrubs, was used by the Pimas for fever, by the Catawbas for back pain and by the Chickasaws for headache and nosebleed. It is the major ingredient in aspirin and an important painkiller. Syrup of ipecac, taken from the root of Cephaelis plants by South Americans, and from Euphorbia, was used by the Creek, Cherokee, and San Carlos tribes to rid the body of impurities. It is still used as an emetic.

Other Native American contributions to our present-day medicine include quinine, morphine, curare, cocaine, morphine, atropine, scopolomine, and hyoscyamine, plus hundreds of lesser-known drugs that are chemically duplicated and can be found today on drugstore shelves.

Throughout this book, the term "Native American" includes those who lived in Canada and other parts of the Americas before Columbus. Medicine men and women are called "healers," even though many of them were primarily shamans, conjurors, sucking doctors or members of healing societies. When it appears that only men were healers, then I refer to them as "medicine men."

Since many Native Americans shared a need for guardian spirits and believed supernatural power came to those who sought visions, this book focuses on healing power derived from these spirits. Native Americans who believed healing power was gained in other ways, most often through inheritance, and who conducted communal cures, are discussed in Chapter 5. It is worth noting that Native American healers could cause illness as well as cure it, even though this book confines itself to their curing powers only.

Finally, some of the plants used to cure common illnesses are examined along with traditional ceremonies and sacred objects used by healers. The herbs listed are not recommended for use but it is exciting to know their secrets because some of them are considered weeds with little or no value.

Today many Native Americans keep their traditions alive by celebrating important events at home and during annual pow wows. Their history is of the past, like all other histories, but their lives are no different than those of other Americans.

FROM THE EARTH TO BEYOND THE SKY

1

Health, Harmony, and Happiness

"The Medicine Wheel Circle is the Universe.
It is change, life, death, birth and learning.
This Great Circle is the lodge of our bodies,
our minds, and our hearts. It is the cycle of
all things that exist."

— Hyemeyohsts Storm, *Seven Arrows*

For Native Americans, the universe was home. Father Sky covered them from above and Mother Earth supported them from below. And between, brothers and sisters shared in the plenty. The largest bear was no more important in this great home than the smallest insect, humans no more important than rocks or mice. In this world, everything depended on something else, and living and nonliving environments flowed together in a giant circle supported and connected by spirits.

Mother Earth's life-giving waters had spirits. Lush green plants had spirits. Even tiny pebbles and ferocious bears had spirits. And beyond Mother Earth's grasp, the wind, sun, rain, stars, and clear blue sky had spirits — spirits that felt love, happiness, pain, hate, joy, sadness, and jealousy.

Infused with spirits that filled them with feeling and wisdom, men, mountains and mosquitos employed supernatural power to keep them connected. This power came from a mysterious force that traveled through the universe, filling everything with energy. It caused many things to happen — seasonal changes, the movement of the sun across the sky, and day turning to night. It wandered along sunbeams, circled rainbows and zigzagged down bolts of lightning. It made sense of the universe. Non–Native Americans came to translate this power into the power of Gods or Great Spirits. Algonquian-speaking tribes call it *manitou;* to Iroquois-speakers, it is *orenda;* to Caddoan-speakers, *tirawa;* and to Siouan-speakers, it is *wakan tanka.*

Spirits, fueled by supernatural power and energy, filled the universe with growth and change. Plants and animals came alive, grew strong and healthy and eventually returned to earth to enrich the soil. Everything in the universe flowed together and everything in the circle renewed its relationship to one another. Native Americans kept these circles tightly linked.

Children learned everything they had to know by listening, watching and imitating adults. They ran errands, gathered firewood, collected wild plants, and gardened. They helped cart household waste outside villages and poured used wash water over the land where it filtered into the soil instead of returning directly to the rivers and streams that gave them drinking water. As they matured, children learned that spirits were all around them — where they lived and where they played.

Native Americans are avid storytellers, and storytelling is one way children learn. Myths, legends, and folktales weave through everyday life like the tough flexible grasses that are curled and twisted into baskets. The storytellers' gestures and voices bring life to their characters. Sometimes they make people laugh, other times gasp and cry. Words wrap themselves around important thoughts. Even silence has meaning. Children hold these pictures in memory. Myths allow the listeners to imagine characters and events they will never see or experience.

Some tales link the past with the present, explaining tribe origins. In the east, these myths and legends often include stories about turtles. Algonquian tribes tell how earth began on the back of a giant turtle that rose out of the sea. On the turtle's back was a small dab of soil. Seeds, carried by the wind, blew over the turtle. Some of them dropped into the soil on the turtle's back and took root. Soon tall plants grew all over the turtle. Their seeds attracted flocks of birds who came to feast. In time, birds' eggs, fish, frogs, nuts, and berries attracted skunks and raccoons. Before long, the turtle's back was an island covered with plants and animals. Then the ancestors of Native Americans came to live there.

Storytellers describe natural events by giving them character. Stories about Ga-oh, Spirit of the Winds, let listeners invent wind images of their own.

Ga-oh was a giant who was confined to the northern skies, which pleased many natives because he would have torn the heavens into pieces if he were loose. At the door of Ga-oh's house, four guards were tied: Bear (North Wind), Panther (West Wind), Moose (East Wind), and Fawn (South Wind). Ga-oh chose these earth creatures to be his guards because they knew the land. When he called Bear to the sky, the huge, lumbering creature pushed aside winds and crossed the mountains to its master's gate. Ga-oh said, "You are strong, Bear; the whole earth can be carried in your arms, and waters will freeze with your cold breath. Go stay in the far north and watch all those winter winds that try to get lost in the sky." Ga-oh led Bear to his place in the northern sky, and said, "You will be my North Wind."

A loud ugly noise that echoed with darkness brought Panther to Ga-oh's side. "You are strong enough to carry winds on your back and water over your shoulders," said Ga-oh. "Go to the western sky, catch the sun trying to hide, and warn the night. You will be my West Wind."

Ga-oh believed he had finished designing the sky and sat down. Suddenly he heard a loud crash and the stomp of heavy hoofs in the forest. Ga-oh looked down and saw Moose looking up. Ga-oh thought Moose well suited to blow strong easterly winds filled with heavy rain over the land. "You have large horns and can make a broad path through the woods," said Ga-oh. "You will be a match for the young clouds that float unchilled over the sky. Go dwell in the eastern sky. You will be my East Wind."

In a gentler voice, Ga-oh called Fawn. Fawn blew in slowly and softly. "You know warm breezes, summer sun, and sunbeams that make the flowers grow. You will bring peace and be known as South Wind."

Except when they had occasional outbursts, Ga-oh and the winds guarding his door were responsible and well behaved. When Ga-oh was happy, wonderful warm, gentle breezes fanned Earth; when he was distressed, cold, angry blasts uprooted trees and blew huge walls of seawater over the land; and when Ga-oh was very restless, wind blew in all directions as he tried to free himself from the confines of the northern sky. Some tribes say that when the north wind blows very strongly, Bear is prowling in the sky; when west winds blow fiercely, Panther is whining; when east winds bring chilly rainstorms, Moose is panting; and if gentle southerly puffs of wind drift up from the south, Fawn is returning to its doe.

Stories about mythological characters teach children how supernatural beings behave and expect to be treated. Characters cavort around the universe, sometimes acting like wild animals and other times like humans. Sometimes they are well behaved and other times they are bad. They could be heroes or tricksters; often they change back and forth in the same story. Mythological creatures are at the mercy of human passions and curiosities and they often get into trouble.

Native Americans lived in many different regions, and their myths and stories include the plants and animals that were important to their way of life. Stories told by hunting tribes were often about the animals they pursued; those of farming tribes were about the earth and weather which they depended on for healthy crops. The adventures of ravens were told by tribes who lived in the Northwest, where ravens make their home; tales of coyotes by tribes who lived on the Great Plains; and tales of rabbits by those who lived in the eastern woodlands.

Algonquian-speaking tribes who live in the east tell of a mythological character named Glooscap, the first man, the Great Spirit, a hero or a trickster. In a tale about

Glooscap and the Baby, Glooscap conquered a race of giants and fought with goblins, witches, and other scary creatures. He strutted around, bragging about his bravery and saying he had nothing left to master. But a woman with a baby heard him and said, "You have not taken care of everyone. There is another mightier than you."

Glooscap asked the name of the mighty person, even though he did not believe the woman. The woman answered, "His name is Wasis, and he is a little baby. But stay away from him." Glooscap found Wasis on the floor of his wigwam, sucking maple sugar and smiling. He asked the baby to come to him, and when he would not, Glooscap imitated a beautiful bird song. Wasis continued to suck on his maple sugar and ignored the song. Glooscap began to rant and rage. His outburst caused Wasis to cry so loudly that he drowned out the angry threats. Glooscap then called upon his magical powers for help. He recited one of his most horrible chants — a call to the dead. But Wasis ignored him.

Finally, Glooscap gave up and rushed out of the wigwam. Wasis, still sitting on the floor and smiling, called after him, "Goo, goo!" Ever since, some Algonquian-speaking tribes say that when their babies say "goo," it means they remember the defeat of Glooscap. Perhaps it gives them courage and daring.

Glooscap was also known to roam the land of the Iroquois, where he appears as an ageless giant with stone eyebrows. The Iroquois tales portray him as kind to humans even when his own life is threatened. In some stories, he is the friend and companion of a tiny forest dwarf named Mikumwesu. Most woodland dwarfs were feared, but Glooscap did not fear Mikumwesu. Instead, he often asked Mikumwesu to help him. The adventures of heroes like Glooscap hold many lessons for children and are still enjoyed by those who hear them.

Tales often changed when passed down through generations. Some grew longer, and others got shorter or were forgotten. Retelling caused stories to change so much that they became "legends" that sound like historical events. And even the legends changed. Some legends became folktales, suitable for people everywhere.

Native Americans understood from their myths, legends, and stories that everything in the universe was alive and filled with feeling and that illness resulted when the spirits felt neglected or offended, when tribal rules were broken, or when people mistreated one another. Everyone tried to be courteous and thoughtful, but sometimes they forgot and the spirits dealt swift punishment.

Angry spirits were blamed for both minor ailments and serious illnesses. Native Americans believed that the best way to get rid of illness was to flush it out of the body. They ate plants raw, sucked their juices, or brewed them in water to induce vomiting, diarrhea, and sweating. But when home remedies did not work, Native Americans took their illness to a professional healer.

2

Plant Medicine

"Mon-o-lah, the earth mother, came to me through my moccasins. I could feel her push and swell here and sway and give there."

— Forrest Carter, *The Education of Little Tree*

Many Native American origin myths tell about plants that cure. The Cherokee people of North Carolina say that long ago plants, animals, and rocks shared a common language and a need to survive. Then humans suddenly began to multiply and act unfriendly toward others. To obtain food and clothing, hunters developed weapons and began to shoot arrows at their defenseless animal brothers. Many animals died, and others ran into the forest to hide.

Eventually, the bears held a council meeting in the forest. Old White Bear said, "We must come out of hiding and defend ourselves. Let us make bows and arrows of our own and fight back." They did, but they could not shoot them because their claws got in the way. "Look, I cut off my claws," said a bear. "Now I can shoot arrows."

Old White Bear shook his head. "Without claws you cannot dig roots, climb trees, or hunt. It is a bad solution." So herds of deer gathered to discuss the problem. They decided that hunters who killed them without first asking permission in the proper way would be punished. Hunters would suffer from pains in their joints for the rest of their lives.

When birds, insects, and reptiles heard what the deer had decided, they also held a meeting. Fish Hawk spoke first. "We will not be so generous to our human brothers and sisters. We will make them very sick. Pain will remind them they are no more important than any other creature."

Plants listened to the angry animals. "Humans are definitely out of harmony with the universe," said Rose Bush, "but should they suffer so much illness? Should they die?" The rest of the plants agreed that illness and possibly death was a harsh solution. Finally Rose Bush spoke again. "Let us try to make up for the anger of our brothers and sisters. Let the plants — the shrubs, grasses, water lilies, and trees of the earth — create cures for illnesses."

Thus, plants and animals worked out an agreement with humans: people could hunt if they asked permission first and gave thanks to the spirit of the giver. But if they forgot and angered the animal spirits into making them ill, then plants would help them recover. This arrangement most affected tribes of hunters, but it was important to every tribe because they all spent some time hunting.

In Canada's James Bay region, hunters asked bear spirits for permission before setting out. They told the spirits that they needed meat for food, fur for clothing, and bones for tools. Then they honored bears at great feasts. They hung their bones, decorated with colored paint, near a lake to please the spirits.

Tribes that spent as much time farming as hunting, like those that lived in the east, held annual ceremonies to return thanks to spirits on this earth and above. One such harvest celebration, called the Green Corn Ceremony, was popular with many groups. During an 1840s celebration, a Native American said, "Great Spirit, continue to listen: we thank thee for thy great goodness in causing our mother, the earth, again to bring forth her fruits. We thank thee that thou has caused Our Supporters to yield abundantly." During the Green Corn Ceremony, all the tribe members danced and sang songs. On the last day of the ceremony they also played games and drank a soup made from corn and beans. A ceremony like the Green Corn was an important way of giving thanks for abundant crops and ensuring success in the coming season. It was also a time when healers conducted curing rituals.

From the mountains, foothills, valleys, coasts, and deserts of North America, Native Americans plucked powerful medicines. They knew the plants that made the best medicines and the best foods. Some plants served both purposes. Herbal teas often relieved headaches, fevers, stomachaches, and joint pains. Plant pastes and salves pulled illness out through the openings of cuts, blisters, and arrow wounds.

Native Americans often made use of plants whose appearance or characteristics seemed related to a specific disease. Liverleaf plant, used to cure liver disease, had leaves shaped like a human liver. Snakeroot plant, which cured snakebite, grows in forests and has long, twisting roots that resemble snakes. Weasel plants, which grow in the desert, are fast-acting like their namesakes, who dig quickly into the ground when startled. Weasel plants speeded childbirth for tribes of the Hopi. Maidenhair fern has fronds, or leaves, that are curled up in the young plant but unroll and straighten as they grow, the way muscles straighten when relaxed. Fern tea relieved muscle and joint pain.

Certain rituals and procedures required gathering herbs and preparing them in a special way. Native Americans collected a few fresh plants of a species, being careful to leave others for later in the season, and handled them carefully. Sometimes they kept the plants out of the sun, and other times they dried plants in the sun to obtain its healing powers. Tribes of the Pequot, who lived in what is now Connecticut, took water from local streams to make tea. Water scooped up against the current induced vomiting; scooped with the current, it induced diarrhea.

Trees, the largest of earth's plants, supplied Native Americans with potent medicine, durable wood, and an unending source of natural materials. Beneath the rough outer bark of the tree is a soft, fibrous layer that moves food and water through it. In the spring, when the inner bark provides the energy for new growth, the outer bark loosens its grip on the tree and is easy to strip. Native Americans collected tree bark in the spring and stored it for later use. During the rest of the year, they made medicines from pieces of bark and used large sheets of bark as splints to set broken bones. They heated and shaped sheets of cedar or birch bark and tied these splints on the injured limbs with rope made from the inner bark of basswood trees. Native Americans also gathered and stored leaves, flowers, stems, sap, and roots from trees to make medicines.

Tribes in different regions used similar plants to treat a wide variety of illnesses. Only a few of the plants used by Native Americans are listed here, and none of them is recommended for use. The scientific name is included in parentheses to help identify common species. The genus is listed first, followed by the species name. When the genus name is the same as the common name, it is abbreviated.

American Holly (*Ilex vomitoria*)

People who lived in low swampy areas along the Atlantic coast collected small three-inch leaves from American holly shrubs. The leaves, also called yaupon, were steeped in hot water and made into a brew called the "black drink." Many tribes dried the leaves and twigs of the plant, put them in clay pots, and parched them over a fire. When boiled, the leaves turned the water very dark. This drink was a powerful stimulant and caused severe perspiring and vomiting. Tribes of the Catawba brewed a similar, but milder, drink using brackish water. The drink restored appetite and cleansed the body. The black drink, still taken during ceremonies when a Seminole becomes a medicine man, contains large amounts of caffeine.

Anemone (*A. canadensis*)

While collecting healthful herbs in open fields, some tribes of the Plains also collected the roots of the anemone plant. These tough, fibrous roots support straight stalks that seldom grow more than a foot high. Tribes of the Omahas and Poncas, who lived on the eastern edge of the Great Plains, crushed the roots and applied the mixture to wounds to speed healing. They also boiled the leaves and made a tea that healed eye infections and lessened body aches and pains. Other tribes crushed the leaves of the plant and made a paste, which they applied to sore joints.

Aster (*A. laevis*)

Tribes who lived in the deserts of the Southwest often went in groups to collect aster plants that grew around seasonal water holes. Asters belong to a large family of delicate wildflowers that set their roots deep in the sand. These flowers supplied Native Americans with an endless amount of healthful herbs. Women made tea from aster leaves and stems to reduce fever and ease joint pain. When the flowers finished blooming, children collected thousands of the tiny seeds, which their families ground into a smooth paste. The paste, applied to the scalp, killed hair lice.

Tribes of the Hopi drank aster tea to reduce cold symptoms and applied damp petals to spider bites to eliminate itching. Other tribes burned dried aster plants and funneled the smoke through a birch bark tube into the nostrils of unconscious patients to revive them.

Cascara Sagrada (*Rhamnus purshiana*)

Along the Pacific coast, from northern California to British Columbia, many tribes collected bark from cascara sagrada trees. These trees often reach a height of sixty feet, but Native Americans looked for them in narrow canyons where they seldom grow more than twenty feet high. They collected quantities of the tree's thick reddish bark, and the women made a brew that acted as a mild laxative. Some tribes believed the bark was most effective if dried and preserved for two years before using. Spanish missionaries admired the gentleness of cascara bark tea and called it "holy bark." By the early 1900s, more than 100,000 trees each year were stripped of their bark, destroying acres of northwestern forest. Cascara sagrada is still used as a laxative today.

Red Cedar (*Juniperus virginiana*)

Few trees could survive the strong winds, intense summer heat and lack of water in some areas of the Great Plains. Red cedar trees are survivors and grow wherever their tough roots can take hold. Though they remain short and stubby, red cedar trees stay green all year, and their twigs, when broken or bruised, smell sweet and fresh. Tribes of the Plains burned cedar twigs and inhaled the smoke when they had head colds. In the mid 1800s, when an epidemic of cholera, a disease brought by the Europeans, swept through the Plains, the tribes obtained some relief by drinking a concoction of red cedar berries and leaves. Red cedar tea induced sweating and soothed joint pain. Red cedar oil is used today as a chemical mixer.

Purple Coneflower (*Echinacea angustifolia*)

Plains Indians, who followed herds of migrating buffalo, often collected the narrow-leaved purple coneflower plants that grow in rich soils. Coneflower stems can grow five feet high, and the large flowers often towered above children's heads. From July through October, Native Americans combed fields, collecting stems, flowers, and roots.

Tribes of the Fox used coneflower roots to cure stomachaches and to quiet convulsions. The Comanche used coneflower tea for sore throats, and other tribes squeezed juice from the stem and rubbed it on burns to promote healing. Sometimes men took the stems to sweat lodges and dripped the juice over hot rocks to reduce the intensity of the heat.

Creosote (*Larrea mexicana*)

Creosote bushes flourish in the light, sandy soils of desert and dry basin regions. These bushes are easy to locate because their stems are black and their leaves green. In some areas of the Mohave Desert, creosote bushes attract many desert rodents, who love to eat the plant's tiny flower seeds.

The fragrant leaves of creosote bushes, when softened in hot water, heal burns and skin wounds. Native Americans used creosote tea for colds and chest congestion. An ointment made by boiling and crushing leaves and branches together eased joint pain and healed painful bruises. Tribes of the Papago boiled creosote leaves and washed fresh wounds with the mixture, while the Pimas and Maricopas boiled creosote branches to extract the oil that they mixed with water and drank to cure stomach pain.

Wild Garlic (*Allium reticulatum*)

Native Americans understood that many plants prevented illness as well as cured it. Wild garlic was eaten raw or cooked throughout the plains to ensure good health. Women boiled the roots of the plant and it was eaten to prevent nose and mouth bleeds, restore energy, aid digestion, and clean out the bowels. Some tribes even applied the plant juice to insect stings.

In the early 1800s, a group of European explorers trekking through the Rocky Mountains suffered from a strange disease that killed many of them. Those who stayed in camp became weak and bled from the nose and mouth before dying, while those who spent their time hunting in the mountains remained healthy. A study of expedition records some years later showed that those who spent time away from the group on hunting trips ate quantities of wild garlic, high in vitamin C.

In 1834, Prince Maximilian, Archduke of Austria, suffered from weakness and bleeding while traveling in the New World. His cook had learned from Native Americans that the prince's illness could be cured by eating wild garlic bulbs, so he gathered a large basketful and cooked them. Within days after eating the garlic, the prince recovered.

Native Americans ate wild garlic and other plants, as well as a variety of animal organs rich in vitamin C to prevent what they called white man's disease, later known as scurvy.

Oregon Grape (*Mahonia aquifolium*)

The warm, moist air that blows in off the Pacific Ocean nourishes many plants and trees. Evergreen trees and shrubs that grow tall and strong along the coast provide shade for many tenacious plants. Oregon grape shrubs were among those that benefited from the shade of coastal evergreens. These six-foot-tall shrubs produce hollylike leaves and small, bright yellow flowers, followed by bluish berries. Native Americans brewed the cut-up roots of the Oregon grape to make a bitter tonic. The Kwakiutls drank Oregon grape tea to dilute bile in the system.

Hemlock (*Tsuga canadensis*)

It is easy to find hemlock trees in northern woodlands because their bluish color sets them apart from their dark green neighbors. Two white stripes on the underside of each tiny hemlock leaf give the branches a silvery glow. Today we use hemlocks as Christmas trees, but years ago Native American women and children collected the leaves and sheets of reddish gray bark for health purposes. Tribes of the Chippewa and Menominee boiled pieces of bark and leaves to decrease fever and relieve upset stomach. Some tribes made a paste from the bark and applied it to wounds, burns, and sores. Tribes of the Penobscot, Montagnai, Micmac, and Menominee drank hemlock tea to rid them of fevers, earaches, and even laziness.

The earliest settlers in the Adirondack Mountains of the Northeast and in Canada discovered that the strong tannic acid in hemlock tree bark could be used to tan leather.

They stripped hundreds of acres of hemlock forests, taking the bark and leaving the trees to decay.

Native Americans enjoyed tea made from hemlock leaves. But European settlers feared the drink, not realizing that it was different from the poisonous one that Socrates swallowed. That lethal brew was made from the European hemlock plant, a small weed with parsleylike leaves that grows in meadows.

Indian Fig, or Prickly Pear Cactus (*Opuntia ficus-indica*)

Another desert plant that many children learned to identify and handle with caution was Indian fig, or prickly pear cactus. This cactus grows throughout desert regions and often reaches a height of fifteen feet. It has thin flat joints that cover the stem and act as leaves. Flowers appear along the joints, followed by large fat fruits. The fruits are covered with fine bristles that make them difficult to handle. Native Americans used a piece of animal hide or a tough leaf to rub away the bristles on the fruit. Though many tribes collected the fruit for food, others cut it up to relieve headache, reduce body swelling, and soothe sore throats. Some groups boiled the juice and drank it to cure respiratory ailments. The fuzz from the outside of the fruit often healed warts and moles.

Jimsonweed (*Datura stramonium and meteloides*)

Many plants that look innocent are actually deadly if eaten. One such plant, jimsonweed, also called devil's apple, mad apple, and stinkweed, holds powerful hypnotic and hallucinogenic alkaloids that can alter a person's ability to make decisions. The plant grows from one foot to ten feet high with thick green-purple stems, large leaves and pale violet or white flowers. Menacing-looking spiny seed pods hold the plant's most deadly drugs.

Luiseños on the Pacific coast and inland Yokuts gave jimsonweed tea to young boys during initiation ceremonies. They remained drugged for almost a month. When the boys recovered, childhood memories had disappeared and they became men. Some tribes ground various parts of the plant into ointments and applied them to sores and wounds to speed healing. The strength of the alkaloids in jimsonweed change each season according to where the plants grow and how much water they receive. Thus, any part or quantity of the plant can be fatal.

Milkweed (*Asclepias speciosa*)

In many areas of North America, summer and fall meadows blossom with milkweed plants that can grow over five feet high. Children waited anxiously for the drooping flower clusters to mature into solid upright seed heads.

When the fat pointed pods were ready to open, the children waved them in the air. Thousands of tiny brown seeds attached to fine white parachutes took off and danced in the wind.

Milkweed plants require careful handling because many of their parts are poisonous. Tribes of the Great Basin collected the stems and used the milky sap to dress wounds and cure ringworm. Others boiled the roots and applied a mushy mixture to the forehead of headache sufferers. Several groups boiled or pounded the roots and applied the mixture to body joints to relieve pain, or to the chest to eliminate coughs. Or they made a mild solution of boiled leaves, stems, and roots and drank the concoction to expel mucus and clear respiratory tracts.

Partridgeberry (*Mitchella repens*)

With their heads bowed, women and children searched northern woodlands for low-growing woody plants called partridgeberries. Trailing along the ground, bright green, heart-shaped leaves cover many forest floors year-round. Small red berries appear beneath a profusion of leaves in late fall and stay to be picked all winter. Partridgeberry leaves steeped in water for tea cured insomnia. Pregnant women drank the tea to guarantee a safe and easy childbirth. As a result, early settlers often called this plant squawberry. Partridgeberry leaves contain tannic acid that makes a refreshing tonic. The berries secrete a soapy foam that dissolves in water and was used as a detergent.

White Pine (*Pinus strobus*)

Another tree that stays green all year is the white pine. It is easy to recognize because it grows very tall and straight, and the clusters of leaves, or needles, grow in bunches of four or five, each leaf from three to five inches long. People soaked the inner bark of pine trees in water and drank the brew to ease pain, swelling, and coughing. Or they placed crushed bark on fresh wounds to quicken healing. Some tribes made tea from new green buds or seed cones to induce diarrhea and soothe joint pains. The strong thick sap of the tree, sometimes mixed with fat, healed boils, ulcers, and other skin wounds.

In 1535, a French explorer named Jacques Cartier became icebound on the St. Lawrence River in Montreal, Canada. During the winter, Cartier lost twenty-five men to an illness that caused nose and mouth bleeds and extreme weakness. One winter day, a group of Native Americans came across the ice to Cartier's ship. Cartier spoke to them but tried to hide his illness. He casually mentioned that he and some of his men had suffered unusual weakness and bleeding. The visitors understood the problem immediately. A group of them went into the forest and collected the leaves and bark of what is believed to have been white pine trees, or perhaps hemlock, and brought them aboard the ship. They told Cartier to boil them in hot water. Cartier and his crew drank the brew and within days regained their health. More than one hundred years later, James Lind, a British surgeon, discovered that Cartier and his men had been dying from lack of vitamin C.

The inner bark of white pine trees also contains tannic acid and other chemicals useful in treating diseases of the lungs.

Raspberry (*Rubus idaeus*)

The raspberry bush bears deep red, sweet-tasting fruits. Raspberry bushes are easy to find because their stems have prickles. Native American women and children collected the delicious berries each summer for food. Chippewa and Menominee women in particular used them to sweeten bad-tasting medicines. People also boiled raspberry root bark in water and made a tea for infected eyes and stomachaches. People today use raspberry juice to flavor foods and neutralize acidity.

Virginia Snakeroot (*Aristolochia serpentaria*)

Along the foothills of the Appalachian Mountains, Virginia snakeroot plants clutch the rich soils of dense woodlands. These shade-loving plants were easy for children to find because their strange-looking leaves grow directly from the root, rise into the air for several inches, then drop toward the ground. The plant's small brownish purple flowers, which bloom in July, are more difficult to find.

Tribes of the Cherokee chewed the plant's root to reduce fevers, toothaches, and colds. Other tribes made tea from the roots to increase appetite, tone up digestion, and eliminate stomach pain. The most popular use is obvious from the name snakeroot. Throughout North America there are many poisonous snakes. When snakeroot plants were not available to cure snakebites, Native Americans cut up the offending snake and placed its flesh over the wound.

Native Americans used hundreds of plant remedies for a variety of ailments. But when illness was too serious for treatment at home, they sought the help of healers who could diagnose and cure illness. These medicine men and women prescribed special herbs as well as healing ceremonies.

3

The Making of a Medicine Man

"The spirits would even whistle. I would be frightened and nervous, and if I remained there I would be molested by large monsters, fearful to look upon. Even the [bravest] might be frightened, I was told."

— Paul Radin, *The Autobiography of a Winnebago Indian*

There is no one way to become a healer: no particular age and no special way for medicine spirits to come. When the time is right, they come. Sometimes they come to women, but most often to men. They might come at puberty or wait until middle age. How and when a person acquires the supernatural powers needed to heal others depends upon the spiritual beliefs of the tribe.

Native Americans who lived in California and other parts of the Northwest and Southwest and in areas of the Southeast believed the power to heal was inherited. Their healing ceremonies and rituals were very different from those of the hunting tribes who lived east of the Rocky Mountains. These tribes felt a need for guardian spirits and believed healing power came to those who sought them.

Guardian spirits were believed necessary to protect and guide adults throughout life. They gave people confidence and encouragement and acted as second identities. Sometimes extraordinary spirits came in place of personal guardian spirits and brought supernatural power that enabled men to become healers. Girls sought guardian spirits if they were given encouragement to do so, but success in feminine pursuits did not require them and women seldom became healers. At puberty, young people, mostly boys, focused on seeking guardian spirits through dreams and visions. Healers had power to confer with the spirit world and move back and forth between it and the material world with ease. They could control and influence troublesome spirits that caused illness and disharmony in the universe. Ordinary guardian spirits did not bring this kind of power.

The most popular way to seek a guardian spirit was to go on a vision quest, a long trip to a special spot in the mountains or forests. Tribal elders usually took young men to a particular location where they stayed alone and fasted for four days. Hunger and loneliness often brought on visions of familiar animals like beaver, bear, moose, elk, deer, raccoon — even mosquitos. If a beaver spirit came, it represented every beaver in the universe and was a guardian for life. Young men hoped their visions would be strong enough to make them great warriors, hunters, chiefs, or healers. Visions that brought supernatural power were meant for healers.

Young men remembered their elders' stories about personal vision quests, of how their hearts and minds raced day and night in anticipation of a vision. The elders told of the noises they heard in the night and of how disappointed they were when faraway sounds echoed and the darkness became suffocating. It was scary to sit alone all night, hungry and cold, listening to strange noises, but the hope of seeing a large, powerful eagle or a whiskered beaver made it worthwhile. Familiar images danced in their heads as they sat and waited. The elders promised that if no vision came, there was no limit to the number of times young men could try for another.

On the plains, young men often sought visions in special squared-off areas marked by colored flags that represented the four cardinal directions: a yellow flag marked east and represented the sun that rises to light the world; a white flag marked south to represent the glare of the sun in its zenith and to suggest snow; a black flag marked west to imply night, darkness, and mystery; and a red flag marked north, to represent earth, pipestone, and the blood of the people. Thin ropes connected the flags. Attached to the ropes, at intervals, were small bundles of tobacco. The spirits adored tobacco, which was offered raw or as smoke. Sometimes vision seekers left little pouches filled with tobacco on tree limbs in the forest where spirits could take them away when no one was looking. It was the gift of a vision seeker happy with his new guardian spirit.

Among tribes of the Miami, who lived in present-day Wisconsin, boys and girls practiced fasting and staying alone at night before they reached puberty. Boys blackened their faces with charcoal, and girls with soil, to show they were going off into the mountains alone. Their first practice quest was an overnight fast. The second time, they stayed two nights. The third, they stayed three nights. When it was time to go away for four days and nights, they had already attracted the attention and pity of supernatural spirits, and visions came quickly.

Creek boys, not girls, who lived in Alabama and Georgia, began their first practice vision quest with a four-day stay in the mountains. If they lasted four full days, their next session was eight days long. If they had a vision during this time, they could go away for a final twenty-day quest. Guardian spirits always encouraged them to go for the full twenty days because each fast increased their spiritual power. Twenty days was a very long time to sit alone, and boys had to be in excellent physical and mental condition to go. Many of these young men later became healers. Tribal elders gave them a buzzard feather to heal arrow wounds, a fox skin for snakebites, and an owl feather to find enemies. They were also entitled to study secret curing songs, dances, and stories.

The guardian spirit of Crazy Horse, warrior chief of the Western Dakota, appeared in a vision as a horse. Crazy Horse said his guardian spirit came from another world, where life forms appeared as shadows. He saw a dancing-shadow horse that cavorted about in a queer way. When the horse disappeared, Crazy Horse knew it was to be his guardian spirit for life. Crazy Horse's vision was stronger than an ordinary vision, and the horse spirit guided him safely through many dangerous battles, but it was not strong enough to make him a healer.

Guardian spirits who brought extra power arrived in the same way as ordinary spirits, but they appeared with greater force. They lingered longer and came back often. Boys who suspected that their guardian spirits were especially powerful took their visions to tribal medicine men to interpret. If the power given by the vision was meant for curing others, they too became healers.

Lame Deer, a nineteenth-century Dakota medicine man, had a powerful vision when he was only sixteen years old. He went to a specially marked, squared-off vision spot and sat for four cold lonely days and nights wrapped only in a blanket. At his side was a sacred pipe filled with tobacco and on his lap a gourd rattle. The rattle held small stones and forty tiny squares of flesh taken from his grandmother's arm. Loved ones often put something of themselves, usually pieces of skin, inside gourd rattles to please the spirits and encourage them to appear. After dark on the last night, Lame Deer felt the soft silkiness of bird feathers brushing his back. First he felt the motion, then he heard someone say: "You are sacrificing yourself here to be a medicine man. In time you will be one . . . You will learn about herbs and roots, and you will heal people . . . A man's life is short. Make yours a worthy one."

The voice faded and Lame Deer felt power surge inside him. He thanked his grandmother for her flesh and for giving him the courage to stay alone and without food for so long.

The next morning Lame Deer went back to his village and described his vision to the tribal medicine man. The medicine man told Lame Deer supernatural spirits had visited him disguised as an eagle. Eagle spirits brought Lame Deer enough power to make him an admired and respected medicine man.

Lame Deer later said about medicine power, "If you are not given it, you won't lie about it, you won't pretend. That would kill you, or kill somebody close to you, somebody you love."

Sometimes guardian spirits did not wait for young men to go on vision quests but presented themselves in dreams or spontaneous visions whether or not they were wanted.

Black Elk, a well-known western Dakota medicine man, was only five years old when spirits chose him. Born in 1863 near the Little Powder River in southeastern Montana, Black Elk was riding his pony along a creek one day when he heard a bird screech. He stopped, stood still, and searched for the bird in the trees. Finally he spotted a fine young kingbird high on a limb overhead. Black Elk poised his bow and arrow in the air and was ready to shoot when he heard the kingbird sing: "The clouds all over are one-sided. Listen! A voice is calling you!"

The words of the kingbird did not make much sense to Black Elk, but the two men who emerged from the clouds above the trees dancing and singing were vivid: "Behold, a sacred voice is calling you; All over the sky a sacred voice is calling." When they got close to Black Elk, they turned around, changed to geese, and flew south. Their song turned to rain, and the sound of their drums to thunder.

For the next few years, voices and visions continued to appear, but Black Elk did not think much about them. When he was nine years old, Man Hip, a tribal elder, invited Black Elk to his tipi. During their visit, a voice outside called Black Elk. When he came out, the voice became silent. Suddenly Black Elk's legs became too weak to hold him up and he had to wobble home.

The next day, Black Elk's legs swelled and he could not walk at all. While lying in bed, he looked through the tipi door and saw the two men from the clouds coming toward him. They beckoned him. "Hurry! Your grandfathers are calling you."

Black Elk slipped out and joined them. They jumped onto a cloud and sailed far away. Before long they came upon a bay horse who called twelve black horses, twelve white horses, twelve sorrel horses, and twelve buckskins to come along. They set off together, four by four, through the sky. Then suddenly the horses changed into earthly animals and vanished. But Black Elk continued until he came upon a large tipi. Inside, six grandfathers sat in a circle facing the door. They appeared to be waiting. Each grandfather spoke to Black Elk. They gave him many things: power to make life, cause destruction, cleanse the wind, and heal anything on earth that was sick. The grandfathers gave him a wooden cup filled with water, and inside the water was the sky. They also gave him a sacred pipe and a bow and arrow.

As Black Elk's cloud floated over his village, he heard

the oldest grandfather singing: "There is someone lying on earth in a sacred manner. There is someone — on earth he lies. In a sacred manner I have made him to walk."

Peering down, Black Elk could see inside his family's tipi. He heard his mother speaking: "The boy is coming to; you had better give him some water." Black Elk's mother was talking to Whirlwind Chaser, a powerful medicine man called upon to cure her delirious son. Whirlwind Chaser rose silently and brought water to Black Elk's lips. He knew Black Elk had visited supernatural spirits during a twelve-day blackout. He also knew eagles would guide and protect Black Elk for the rest of his life and that Black Elk could become a powerful medicine man.

Black Elk continued to behave like other boys, though his vision recurred year after year and became more complicated each time. He was sad that his mother and father did not know how far he traveled in his visions.

Dakota custom required that Black Elk tell the story of his vision before he put its power to use. When he was eighteen years old he danced and chanted the story in a ritual performed before members of the tribe. When he finished, his power came alive and he could heal others.

In California, a man returned from hunting with a bloody nose and mouth. He said he had seen two sets of deer tracks which converged near a rock, where he found deer droppings and animal hair. Beyond the rock, he came face to face with two condors, huge birds with red-striped beaks and gigantic wings. Then he passed out. When he awoke, he went home and told his family and friends what had happened. Elder tribesmen understood that when the young man passed out, spirits disguised as condors brought medicine power. Following tribal custom, the elders built him a special dance house to honor him as a medicine man.

Along the Skeena River in British Columbia, a thirty-year-old man was out chopping wood when he heard a loud bang overhead. Shortly afterward, he passed out. While unconscious, he had a vision of a great owl flying through a loud, crashing thunderstorm. When he woke, he went home and told his parents what had happened. They put him to bed and called in two medicine men who asked the young man about the crash in the woods and the vision that followed. They listened quietly. Then one of them told the family that spirits had brought the young man medicine power. When he recovered, the young man studied medicine songs for one year and fasted and dreamed on and off for a second year. Finally, he was called upon to cure a sick person whom other medicine men could not heal. The young man's efforts proved successful and he became a respected medicine man.

Sometimes families were so eager for their sons to become healers, they sent them to live with tribal medicine men. Among tribes of the Cherokee, medicine men raised boys who appeared to have the necessary qualifications:

sensitivity, introspection, and caring. Girls did not become healers. Young boys who went to live with medicine men were serious and well behaved. They stayed away from other children who might distract them from learning and watched and helped during healing ceremonies. They seldom spoke because they knew unasked questions would be answered if they waited.

Boys learned that healers had the power to diagnose and cure illness by deciding which ceremony was needed, prescribing the appropriate herbs and knowing whether the disease had to be sucked out of the body. If patients had lost their spirits, healers retrieved them.

Curing rituals required healers to get in touch with their inner powers and connect with the supernatural. Some healers needed to drink herbal brews to accomplish this, but most did not. Healers recited chants and danced, repeating the same words and motions over and over again. They often began to dance facing east, the direction of the rising sun, and proceeded toward the south, west, and north. They moved slowly and rhythmically, chanting in low, monotonous tones as they circled. They told the story of their curing ritual as they danced. If they named the spirit that caused the illness in the songs they sang, the power of their ritual increased. And if they danced in imitation of that spirit, it gained even more power. Eagle spirits might push a healer's body forward and backward and make his arms flutter up and down in long, flapping motions. Bear spirits might make him hunch over and, as he circled, thump firmly on the earth with heavy, forceful steps. These rituals were reenactments of familiar myths known to the audience. Myths about eagles or bears played in memory while the medicine man danced and chanted. Chanting, dancing, and drumming helped connect the audience and patient with the supernatural.

Healers had special herbs and cures known only to them. Sometimes plants made themselves known and medicine men went directly to where they grew.

Black Elk once searched for a sacred herb he saw in a vision. When he found it, he offered tobacco to the six powers of the universe: north, south, east, west, sky, and earth. Then he turned to the plants and said: "Now we shall go forth to the two-leggeds but only to the weakest ones, and there shall be happy days among the weak."

Plants, like humans, live in tribes, and their chiefs require as much respect as those of animal spirits, although plant spirits seldom get angry enough to cause illness.

Healers made offerings to plant chiefs and explained to plant tribes the reason they must be collected. They thanked plants by leaving tobacco for them in a hole next to where they grew. Besides using the plants to help cure patients, medicine men sometimes asked plant spirits to be helpers, although plant spirits had less healing power than animal spirits.

Among the Dakota Indians, who lived in Minnesota and

Wisconsin, healers sometimes changed themselves into plants to learn about curing. One healer dreamed he was a seed with wings, from a milkweed or cattail, blown by the four winds. In the dream, he blew around, listening to the chants, dances, and rituals conducted on earth by tribal medicine men. When the dreamer knew enough, he planted himself inside a pregnant woman. The woman's baby grew up like other children but had the power and wisdom of a medicine man.

Tribes of the Chippewa, who lived around the Great Lakes, employed sucking doctors, who did nothing but remove disease-causing objects from patients by sucking them out with a bone tube. Men who dreamed about a special healing hut and built it according to dream instructions became conjurors. The hut they built was shaped like a small wigwam. It was framed with poles and covered with skins or mats. The conjuror went inside the wigwam and waited for spirits to come through an opening at the top. Outside, members of the tribe sat listening to the conjuror confer with the spirits. The conjuror asked many questions, some of them about the causes of illness. Wigwams often shook violently when spirits came to visit, which is why the ceremony is called "shaking tent." After the spirits left, the wigwam stopped shaking and the conjuror came out with cures for patients.

It was often difficult to tell the difference between healers and other members of the tribe unless tribal custom set them apart. Many healers looked and acted like others until they began to conduct curing ceremonies. Then they took control and acted with such confidence and assurance that there was no question they had special powers.

Sometimes when healers died, their power stayed buried with them until it was needed by someone else in the family. When the time came for a family member to become a healer, the power reappeared once again, even if it had been buried for many generations.

The role of a healer or medicine man was very important in a world filled with active spirits and spirit power. Healers were admired, respected, and feared. They and other members of their tribe believed in their special curing powers. Thankful relatives and families of recovered patients often repaid healers with food, animal skins, clothing, or other valuables.

Yet not everyone wanted to be a healer. Curing could be dangerous business. Patients who died in spite of healers' efforts sometimes had vengeful relatives. Then the healers feared for their lives. Fortunately, this did not happen often. Patients believed in and honored tribal healers as important ingredients in the curing process.

4

Ceremonies and Sacred Objects

"Tribal culture culminated in ceremony, and
to be instructed in ritual and ceremony was to
be an historian of the tribe."

— Luther Standing Bear, *Land of the
Spotted Eagle*

Native Americans believe supernatural spirits are reasonable and approachable and give many celebrations in their honor. Each tribe has its own special way of appealing to the spirits and giving thanks to them. Agricultural tribes hold celebrations during the winter and summer solstices to honor the weather spirits, and hunting tribes hold celebrations to honor the animals they hunt, to give thanks to spirits both on this earth and above for good fortune, and to ask for renewal in the coming year.

In many regions, small groups of Native Americans moved from one location to another, hunting, fishing, gathering wild plants, and gardening in season. They got together at different times of the year to celebrate important events in their lives. They enjoyed singing, dancing, eating, and socializing. They also looked forward to tribal healing ceremonies.

Every ingredient of a healing ceremony had to be just right. Sometimes healers danced slowly in circles. Chanting, dancing, and circling helped them get in touch with their inner healing powers and prepared them for a supernatural journey. Their chants sounded like conversations with the drums and rattles, and they danced to please the spirits with whom they conferred. Their bodies radiated with an energy which was so strong it caused them to rock, sway, and shift in every direction. The steady hypnotic beat of drums and rattles, the monotonous sounds of curing chants and dancing moccasins, helped medicine men lift their minds out of their bodies. It also calmed their patients and held the audience's attention. When the medicine men's minds finally fell back into their bodies, chants trailed off, rattles rasped softly, and drums turned to muffled silence. Spirits gave medicine men the cures they sought.

Tribes of the plains held elaborate Sun Dance ceremonies and tribes who lived in the east and southeast hosted Midwinter and Green Corn ceremonies. At first, Sun Dance ceremonies focused on preparing hunters and warriors to be brave and included only a few curing rituals. Eventually, as the lives of the people changed and buffalo disappeared, Sun Dance celebrations became more focused on healing.

Tribes of the plains often included clowns in curing ceremonies. Clowns poked fun at ceremonial leaders and made people laugh. Clowning often helped to relieve tension during difficult moments.

Iroquoian-speaking tribes (Onondaga, Seneca, Oneida, Mohawk, Cayuga, and Tuscarora) who live in present-day New York State hold a series of midwinter ceremonials in January or February. The start of these ceremonies coincides with the new moon of midwinter. Special messengers wearing buffalo robes tied on with cornhusks and braided cornhusk ankle bands carry pestles from house to house, stirring ashes and announcing the beginning of the celebration. The first few days are devoted to renewal and fulfillment of dreams and are conducted by members of special medicine societies who have limited healing powers.

The Iroquois often analyzed dreams to find cures for sickness. When people slept, their spirits traveled the universe. When they woke up, memories of their travels were unforgettably real and vivid. They believed the vision of their dream was a reflection of their physical and mental needs. Some dreams were harmless, others were not. When a person became very ill, dream interpreters were called upon. These specialists knew by listening to a sick person's dream what curing ritual was needed. Sometimes patients became ill after they dreamed about something they wanted to do or have. Unfulfilled dreams could cause depression, sadness, or unusual fear. Healers understood this and created elaborate ceremonies that encouraged dreamers to act out their dreams to restore health and to prevent illness from recurring.

A Cayuga tribesman once dreamed he ate human flesh. When he told his dream to members of the tribe they agreed he must eat flesh to prevent illness and to ward off bad luck. A young man was found to sacrifice and was brought to the dreamer, who suddenly remembered he had dreamed about a woman. When a woman was about to be put to death, the dreamer cried out, "I am satisfied;

my dream requires nothing further."

Another time, a tribesman dreamed that he burned a Frenchman. The healer knew that in order for the sick man to get better, he must find a Frenchman to sacrifice. When he did, the patient ripped off the Frenchman's coat and threw it into the fire. When the coat had turned to ashes, the patient announced that his dream was satisfied and he felt better.

Iroquois medicine societies often conducted curing rituals that were revealed in a patient's dream. The ritual was reenacted by members, many of whom had been cured themselves by the society. One of the most important curing societies was called Shake the Pumpkin, which owned special masks. Others included the Bear, Otter, Eagle, Buffalo, and Pygmy societies. Each had special origin myths, songs, and rituals and met in private homes. The most powerful society belonged to the Senecas and was called the Little Water Society. This group conducted annual ceremonies to preserve the strength of secret remedies called "little-water powders," which were kept in medicine bundles. Little-water powders were made from ground-up animal parts mixed with water. The society met on the fifth night of the new moon in summer to sing over the bundles and renew their healing powers. Both men and women were members.

Masks were important objects in the rituals of the Iroquois people, and the False Face Society used many of them. Membership in the society was a privilege, and not everyone in the tribe qualified. Women did not belong, but they directed the society's activities, took charge of costumes and participated in a ceremony that enabled them to carry the society's insignia: a pole decorated at the top with miniature False Face and Corn Husk masks and a tiny turtle shell rattle.

The origin of the False Face Society is told through a tale about the Creator, who made it possible long ago for members to own masks that cured or warded off illness and disease.

Long ago the Creator came to earth. He met a spiritual being named Hadu'i', a very conceited personage who bragged to the Creator that he had great power over the creatures of the earth and that it was he who had designed nature. He claimed to be both the maker and ruler of life.

The Creator thought Hadu'i' was terribly arrogant, so he challenged him to a contest. Hadu'i' was angered when the Creator asked him to prove his power by moving a mountain. Hadu'i' tried to move it but could not. The Creator waved his hand, and the mountain shook, trembled, and then moved. Frustrated, Hadu'i' spun around and tripped on a rock. He hit the rock with such force that his nose broke, his mouth turned crooked, and his tongue hung between his teeth. The Creator looked at Hadu'i's distorted face and decided that he would make it permanent, to remind Hadu'i' that arrogance and boasting were dangerous, especially when there were others more powerful.

Although the Creator could have ended Hadu'i's life, he let him live on the condition that Hadu'i' help earth creatures drive out illness and disease.

Hadu'i' hid in a forest cave. When a weary hunter approached, Hadu'i' let out a loud moan. The hunter heard the sound and went to the mouth of the cave to see what had made the noise. Inside, he saw a giant monster with a distorted face. The monster, who was Hadu'i', told the hunter that evil spirits had overcome him and had made him sick and weak. He asked the hunter to go to a tree and carve a mask of his face. Hadu'i' stood outside the cave, instructing the hunter as he carved. When the hunter was done, Hadu'i' told him to go back to his village and use the mask to help heal sick people. From then on, Hadu'i' was called the helper, or our grandfather. Hadu'i' and the hunter who carved the mask started the False Face Society.

At first, all False Face masks resembled Hadu'i', but later they were carved in the form of animals or forest spirits that appeared in dreams. Carvers went into the forest and picked a suitable tree for carving, usually a basswood. Tribesmen guarded chosen trees against evil spirits until the eldest False Face member arrived to begin the proper carving ceremony. Society members burned tobacco at the tree's roots, and the smoke transferred the healing powers of the living tree to the mask and its carver. Also, they rubbed the bark of the tree with a turtle shell rattle. In this way, members absorbed power from the Above World, represented in the tree by its strong branches, which reached toward the sky. The rubbing also absorbed power from the tree's roots, which grew deep in the earth and rested on the back of Turtle Earth. While the carvers worked, members asked the tree to give its spirit life to the mask being carved. They also told the story of Hadu'i'.

When carvers began making a mask in the morning, they painted it red; when they began in the afternoon, they used black paint. Strips from the inner bark of basswood trees served as hair on the first False Face masks. After the seventeenth century, carvers began to use horsehair instead.

False Face members believed that the spirits of their masks controlled what they did and said and gave wearers powerful spiritual and healing powers. Members handled their masks carefully. False Face members performed Midwinter curing rituals in patients' homes, where they danced and called on Hadu'i' for help. In fall, they performed cleansing rites in which they went from house to house, prowling in corners, looking underneath beds, making loud noises, jostling sick people, playing practical jokes on lazy villagers, and throwing ashes around rooms.

These antics were intended to drive unwanted spirits and disease from the home.

Among tribes of the Chippewa, special ceremonies were often conducted by communal curing societies that gave its men, but not women, limited healing powers. The largest medicine society was the Midewiwin, or Medicine Lodge, whose activities were secret. Midewiwin members preserved herbal recipes to pass from one generation to another. Members believed that if they followed the society's rules of conduct and took prescribed herbal concoctions they would enjoy a long, happy life.

The society originated among tribes of the Menominee, Potawatomi, Sauk, Fox, Kickapoo, and Winnebago, who lived west and south of the Great Lakes. Tribes of the Chippewa, who lived north of Lakes Huron and Superior, created a Midewiwin group in the early 1900s. They kept most of the original rituals and added a few. Non–Native Americans got information about the society from non-members and relatives of members.

Each spring and fall, Midewiwin members built special barrel-shaped medicine lodges covered with cedar boughs for initiation ceremonies. On initiation day, candidates hung gifts for members on ridgepoles in front of the lodges. They entered from doorways facing east and sat in the center of a large circle marked by stakes. Midewiwin members marched around the outside carrying medicine bags, tobacco, and food. Before going inside, they left some tobacco on a rock at the entrance. Then they took seats in the circle behind the candidates. An important segment of the initiation ceremony involved telling stories and interpreting the symbols on the society's scrolls, large pieces of birchbark with images of Midewiwin activities. One such surviving scroll pictures two rows of round-headed men facing each other across a large table, four on each side. Above the top row of men, two circles represent the sun and another planet, probably Venus; below the bottom row of men are two underworld monsters sitting side by side.

Shell shooting was part of each initiation ceremony. Society members took small clam shells from their medicine bags, which they threw, or shot, at candidates. The shells were believed to have the power to drive away illnesses. At the conclusion of the ceremony, candidates received personal medicine bags containing the same type of shells that were used in the ceremony.

After initiation, candidates were tested to find out how many plants they could identify and turn into healing medicines. Keen knowledge and understanding of medicinal plants was necessary to gain membership. Midewiwin members kept the names and locations of healing plants a secret, revealing only one at a time to candidates who qualified. To confuse nonmembers, they called one plant by several names and even disguised its odor by smothering it with sweet-smelling herbs.

Men who became healers often owned medicine bundles that held sacred objects with mysterious powers. The power of these objects was transferred to the healer himself. No one else could peer inside the bundle or touch his objects. In the eastern woodlands, medicine bundles made from whole animal skins held great power.

The Winnebago, who lived around the Great Lakes, believed that long ago otter spirits had carried a dead boy back to the real world and made him live. Thereafter, otters were considered sacred animals, and their skins became pouches which were used to hold other sacred objects. The pouches included the skull, legs, and tail of the animal whose natural life was replaced with spiritual objects important to healers. These medicine bundles often also held herbs, tobacco, sucking tubes or sticks, crystal rocks, feathers, claws, bone syringes, and tiny stone, bone, or wooden animal figures that represented the owner's guardian spirit.

Winnebago medicine men spread tobacco on patients and sang songs to force evil spirits from the body. Dakota medicine men placed small pouches filled with tobacco around patients to attract angry spirits. When patients recovered, they took the tobacco into the forest to give the bad spirits a chance to escape.

Many healers did not own medicine bundles but had sacred objects, such as pieces of transparent quartz, which allowed them to see inside the body. Pure crystals with six sides were particularly valuable and brought great power. If transparent pieces of quartz were not available, however, healers used a milky white rock containing quartz crystals.

A healer's power was tested by playing games that required them to see through another's hand. In one such guessing game, the players sat in a large circle with their fists closed. Only one person held a marked animal bone. Healers walked the circle and guessed who held the bone. Such games generally included two six-member teams sitting opposite each other. One team member hid the bone, and a "pointer," or healer, who had power to see, pointed to the holder. Variations on the game involved individuals instead of teams, and stones instead of bones. This game was once so popular that some teams bet horses, wives and even a winter's supply of food on the ability of their healers to guess correctly.

Feathers were also sacred items that enabled healers to detect the location of illness. Healers passed them several inches above a patient's body, from head to foot, to pick up signs of illness in the form of energy, vibrations, or hot spots emanating from the body. When illness was located, it was gathered into a pile by the feather and imaginary slashes made with a sharp stone knife. Healers sucked away the illness, spitting out fluids as they did so. Since they did not actually cut into the patient's body, they created fluids of their own. They often put "spirit helpers" in the form of tiny pieces of wood, bone, shell, or eagle or bear claws under their tongues before they performed a sucking procedure. These helpers caught diseases and held them so they would not enter the healers' bodies. Healers sucked and vomited, sucked and vomited, and between bouts sang curing songs and talked to spirits. Afterward, they took the helpers out of their mouths, showed them to patients and had them buried deep in the ground, far from the village, to prevent spirits from returning and causing any more illness.

The largest of all sacred items was the sweat lodge. Long ago it was used to cleanse mind and body and spiritually prepare men for sacred celebrations and events. Sweat lodges were used mostly by men, but women were the ones who kept them filled with steam. They were dome-shaped and seldom more than four feet high. They had frames made of willow saplings and were covered with bark, grass, animal skins, and mats. Doors faced east, the direction of the rising sun. Men sat inside, around a large pile of hot stones, and poured cold water over them to create intense steam. They would see who could stay the longest, despite the heat.

Chippewa medicine men often stuck cedar boughs among the rocks in sweat lodges to create the smoldering aroma of cedar during sweat baths. The heat of sweat lodges often induced an artificial fever and forced illness out of a patient's body through open pores. Many tribes believed that steam baths should be followed by a plunge into an icy cold stream, but they were very careful, as they knew that extreme temperature variations could be fatal.

5

Other Healers

"In the native American tradition, diseases and
their cures are inseparable from the larger scheme
of things. Medicine is a ritual matter, most
intricately so in the case of the Navajo Ways."

— Gordon Brotherson, *Images of the New World*

The Pueblo, Navajo, California, and Northwest Coast people have distinct spiritual beliefs that make their medicine rituals very different from those practiced among hunting tribes. They seldom need guardian spirits and believe supernatural power is inherited or comes from a powerful dream. They share the belief that angry spirits cause illness by putting stones, thorns, sticks, and strings inside the body. But they share little else. Each group has a well-defined spiritual life and very different healing rituals. The people treat ordinary ailments with herbal remedies; their tribal healers treat serious illnesses. Some groups mix several plants together to make strong brews and others prescribe a single plant for each ailment.

Pueblo healers used inherited supernatural powers to cure both individuals and large groups. During ceremonies they often sprinkled sacred pollen, cornmeal, and tobacco on objects and dancers to feed generous supernatural spirits and keep their powers alive.

The Hopi, a Pueblo group who live on mesas in northern Arizona, conduct ceremonies during the summer and winter solstice. Because they are farmers, weather is important to their survival, and this is reflected in their ceremonies. During the winter solstice, they conduct ceremonies to force the sun, which is at its most southerly position on the horizon, to return north so that crops can grow.

Kachinas, supernatural cloud beings that bring rain, appear at this time and stay until the summer solstice, when they are believed to return to their mountain homes. During these two celebrations, healing societies carry out special curing rituals. Long ago, during the summer solstice, members of the Snake Clan ran into the desert to collect rattlesnakes. They piled the snakes into large pottery jars and placed them in a ceremonial chamber, or kiva, for two days. After the second day, the clan members reached into the jars with their bare hands and grabbed a snake, holding it close to its head so it would not coil and strike. Few medicine men appeared to be hurt by the snakes they pulled from the jars. Perhaps the snakes bit each other while packed together and exhausted their venom, or maybe the men became immune to snake bites by having endured them since childhood. When all the snakes were in a pile on the ground, the men quickly covered them with cornmeal so they could not see to attack. Eventually, the snakes slithered off into the desert, carrying angry spirits with them. This ceremony cleansed the community of bad spirits and ensured good health for the remainder of the year.

The Acoma people, another Pueblo group, live in west central New Mexico. They depended on a variety of healing societies to conduct curing ceremonies. Patients chose a society to cure them and sent a relative to ask members to come to their homes and perform a curing ritual. The relative took special feathers or prayer sticks, which were messages to the spirits, to entice members. If they accepted, they prepared a sacred table in the patient's home. (If they declined, the patient had to choose another society.)

On the sacred table they put an ear of corn, bowls filled with herbal mixtures, gourd dippers, and a quartz "seeing crystal." When everything was ready, the patient came into the room and stretched out on the floor. The head of the society took the quartz crystal from the table and looked into the patient's body to see what made him ill. Other members made separate examinations. Without consulting one another, they diagnosed the illness and took turns treating the patient. Some members massaged the patient to get the illness out; others whipped the disease with an eagle feather; still others sucked it out with a special sucking device. At the conclusion of the ceremony, members washed their hands and gargled with an herbal mixture. Then they asked each member of the family to take a drink. In return for the healing ritual, the family offered cornmeal, flour, blankets, meat, wool, and other valuable articles to society members.

The sacred table and two members of the society remained in the house with the patient for four days. When patients recovered from cures administered by curing societies, they often joined the society themselves.

The Navajo belong to a group of northwestern Athabascan-speaking people who moved to the Southwest in the 1500s. They were neither farmers nor hunters but raiders and sheepherders. Much of their spiritual life is based on traditions formed in a very different environment, and their ceremonies focus on keeping in harmony with the universe. But the Navajo adopted many traditions from their neighbors, especially the Hopi, and this is reflected in their ceremonies.

The Navajo celebrate a variety of dramatic ceremonies, called Chants, to cure serious illness. Navajo healers diagnose illness and then prescribe the appropriate ceremonial cure. But they themselves do not do the curing. Instead, the sick person's family hires a Singer to conduct the ceremony in a special house. The Singer outlines with a stick on the sandy floor of the healing house the story of the curing ceremony that has been specified by the healer. Sometimes stories include important Navajo spirits.

Night Chants, which lasted nine days, purified patients and put them back in harmony with the universe. During the first few days of the chant, patients took sweat baths, attended afternoon prayer stick programs, and sang songs each evening. Prayer sticks were messages to the spirits. During the fourth through sixth days of the ceremony, members of the tribe worked eight to ten hours daily, filling in with colored clay and charcoal the Singer's designs. When they finished, the patient came to the house and sat on top of the sand paintings. While the Singer chanted, he picked up handfuls of the colored sand and placed them on the sick body to take away the illness. Other members of the tribe also chanted during the ceremony, but only the Singer's chant had the power to cure. It was very important that the Singer recite the chants word for word, or their curing powers would not work. When the chants ended, the patient got up from the sand painting and went home. The helpers removed the clay and charcoal from the sandy floor and returned it to the outdoors.

On the morning of the last day of Night Chant, patients washed their bodies and hair in suds made from yucca roots. In the evening, masked dancers appeared to signal the end of the ceremony. Everyone who helped with Night Chant rituals benefited from the cures they brought. If no cure resulted from the chant, the patient understood that it was because some part of the ritual had been omitted or the chant had been repeated incorrectly by the Singer.

The Navajo people also conduct Holy Way Chants to cure illnesses caused by animals and bad weather; Life Way Chants for bodily injuries; Mountaintop Way Chants for contact with bears; Evil Way Chants for sickness caused by ghosts; Blessing Way Chants to ensure health and happiness; and Enemy Way Chants to protect warriors from sickness. Other chants protect the tribe from witches, lightning, or mistakes made by Singers who forgot the words of their chants.

Native Americans who lived in California were neither farmers nor hunters but gatherers and fishermen who had abundant quantities of natural food. Healers did not seek personal guardian spirits but acquired special healing power from dreams and by inheritance. Women often inherited power from close relatives who had been healers. The Shasta, who lived on the California-Oregon border, believed that dead relatives had put tiny pieces of wood, bone, claw, or shiny rocks containing supernatural powers into the mouths of healers.

The Karok people, who lived in northwestern California, employed women sucking doctors. Women became healers after they had spent an unusual amount of time alone in the mountains singing, fasting, and pleading with spirits for curing power.

A male healer of the Achomawi people, who also lived in northwestern California, asked patients to stretch out on the ground with their heads facing east, the origin of light, while he sang and danced around them. During the dance, members of the tribe talked and joked with one another. Then, without warning, the healer began to speak in a loud voice. This meant he had connected with the supernatural and was conferring with spirits. The audience became quiet and eyes riveted on the healer, who continued to sing and dance. Finally his head dropped and his tone returned to normal. But now he spoke so fast that no one could understand him. A companion who stood nearby interpreted. The interpreter's job was to keep the healer in touch with both the audience and the supernatural. He did this by repeating slowly and calmly the healer's words.

Several decades ago, a popular Pomo healer named Essie Parris, who lived with her people in California, discovered healing power in her right hand and throat when she was only thirteen years old. In a desperate attempt to help heal her sister, Essie placed her right hand on her sister's head, and a song came out of her mouth. Essie did not know where the song came from nor what it meant.

Said Essie, "But I didn't sing it out loud; it was singing down inside of me. To my amazement she got well a few days afterward." A non-Indian suffering from pneumonia was cured when Essie touched his chest with her right hand. Essie said the man's disease pulled her hand forward, and she had to hold her breath so the disease would not hide itself. "It is just like when you cast for fish and the fish tug at your bait — it feels like it would with the fish pulling your line. The pain sitting somewhere inside the person feels like it is pulling your hand toward itself — you can't miss it. It lets you touch it," said Essie.

Essie also noticed something in her throat which sucked away pain. At first it appeared as a large growth that interfered with breathing and swallowing. But when the growth got smaller and her breathing returned to normal, she could use her throat to suck away pain. Something like a large bubble came out of Essie's throat the first time she sucked pain from a sick person. Essie spit the illness into her hand and held it out to view. It stayed glued to her hand like a magnet until she buried it along with the angry spirits it held. When she sucked disease from a person's body, Essie heard these words: "This is the way it is. It is [such and such a kind of disease]. This is why."

Northwest Coast tribes believed medicine spirits could be passed after death from father to son or from uncle to nephew, but never through females. Sons and nephews who inherited these healing powers often sought additional power on their own. They took walks in the woods and called spirits to come and help them. Most of the time these spirits brought additional power. Then the young men put on masks they had inherited and danced to show other members of the tribe that they had healing power.

Among the Haida, who lived in the Queen Charlotte Islands in British Columbia, men who inherited medicine spirits set themselves apart from other members of the tribe by wrapping themselves in special blankets. They also carried rattles and rhythm sticks to show their power. Sometimes they grew long hair and kept it uncombed and unwashed. When these men wore their inherited masks, spirits controlled what they did and said. Sometimes spirits spoke strange languages through the mouths of the masks.

The medicine men of the Tlingit, neighbors of the Haida, passed to sons and nephews before they died, secret herbal cures, the names of their guardian spirits, and special ways to increase supernatural power.

Among Salish-speaking groups who lived along the Pacific coast in western Washington State, people suffered from illness and depression when their personal guardian spirits left them. Often spirits left because people squandered money or property. Medicine men had the power to retrieve lost spirits, and patients went to them for help.

It was customary for a group of medicine men to take "spirit canoes" into the Lowerworld to retrieve lost spirits. Journeys began in specially marked holes on house floors, in the stumps of trees or at the entrances to hot springs. Lowerworld holes had tunnels that led to inviting green fields and forests where supernatural creatures lived. Medicine men stayed in the Lowerworld until they had conferred with spirits, then came back through the tunnel and emerged where they entered. Journeys to the Lowerworld always began at night in a house filled with spectators. Medicine men lined up in two single lines, each of which represented an imaginary canoe. The bow person directed the canoe while the stern person kept it on course. Long seven-foot poles, held by each man, served as paddles. Singing and rattle-shaking always accompanied travelers into the Lowerworld. Most journeys lasted two nights. The first night the canoes went all the way to the Lowerworld: the second night, they returned with the lost guardian spirit. Sometimes a trip to the Lowerworld took a week or more. Then paddlers slept during the day and traveled at night. Each evening they resumed their journey wherever it had ended the previous night. Medicine men cured patients according to instructions from Lowerworld spirits. When patients got their spirits back, they stood up and danced around the room to show they were well again.

Conclusion

"You understand that there are certain things one should not talk about, things that must remain hidden. If all was told . . . there would be no mysteries left, and that would be very bad. Man cannot live without mystery. He has a great need of it."

— John (Fire) Lame Deer, *Lame Deer: Seeker of Visions*

Native American healing practices are so closely bound to spiritual beliefs that treatment of physical symptoms is never isolated from the spirituality of the patient. And Native American spirituality has been poorly translated into written languages. Each tribe's spiritual life was unique, creating a variety of healing methods.

Long before Columbus discovered the New World, Native Americans practiced preventive, holistic, and psychiatric medicine. Herbs were used to treat specific bodily ailments but were seldom considered effective without ceremonies for spirits.

Native Americans had an understanding and appreciation for the medicinal properties of plants, as evidenced by the many uses they made of local herbs. They also understood that disease is contagious and can be prevented. Many Native Americans routinely burned down a house in which someone had died. William Bartram, an eighteenth-century medical botanist from Philadelphia, observed the Creek sanitizing villages by burning worn-out clothing and unwanted debris in a giant bonfire.

Native Americans believed strongly in personal hygiene and washed regularly in lakes and streams, regardless of the cold. They also participated in sweat baths that cleansed both body and mind. Europeans, on the other hand, wore layers of heavy clothing that they never removed no matter how warm the weather. Native Americans preferred to be partially exposed rather than fully clothed, inviting the possibility of parasites and disease. Today, steam rooms, saunas, and Jacuzzis often serve the purpose of sweat baths.

Native American healers performed surgery and used a variety of narcotics to ease the pain. They even used sphagnum moss to absorb excess body fluids. Moss and cattail seeds, also used as disposable diaper material, replaced cotton surgical bandages in Montreal factories during World War I. Native American women who worked in the factories suggested the use of moss, and factory owners tested it. They found it could absorb twenty times its weight, while cotton absorbed only six times. Sphagnum moss also worked three times faster than cotton.

Native Americans recognized the need for spiritual harmony and often put patients back in tune with the natural world by using advanced mental health methods. Healers understood and dealt with psychological problems on a regular basis. They conducted ceremonies for patients who felt rejected, depressed, or suffered from severe bouts of fear, anxiety, and tension. Their rituals were both personal and caring and often involved entire families and friends in the healing process. An outpouring of sympathy and affection helped patients feel better about themselves. Today group therapy sessions often accomplish the same thing.

By 1820 it was apparent to physicians that they needed to compile a list of prescription drugs to be used as a common resource. That year a group of them met in Washington, D.C., and drew up a list of useful drugs, including those learned from Native Americans. The list, later known as the United States Pharmacopeia (USP), included formulas, doses, and prescriptions required to cure specific ailments. At first this list was updated every ten years. Now it is updated every five years. A second list, called the National Formulary (NF), was developed in 1888 by the American Pharmaceutical Association, and included drugs that had been dropped from the USP, sometimes because they were not considered effective enough.

More than 170 drugs still listed in the USP and the NF come from tribes who live north of Mexico. And 50 additional drugs come from tribes who live in Mexico, South and Central America, and the West Indies.

Few people today think of plants as drugs, even when they drink herbal tea to soothe aching joints or help them sleep. Herbal teas, skin creams made from aloe plants, and other natural products are popular because many people are attracted to a return-to-nature lifestyle.

For hundreds of years, European physicians treated the whole body in a holistic approach to curing. But science changed what was known about the human body, and healing practices became very specialized. In recent years,

New Age healers have tried to return to holistic practices and have included the mind as well as the body in their methods. Their philosophy has provided a basis for different approaches to curing which go beyond drug treatment. Some practices are particularly popular with people trying to overcome chemical drug dependency or with those who have had no success with conventional treatment. Some of these new techniques include: altered states of consciousness, hypnotherapy, meditation, and stress-reduction therapy. Many also include participation by families and friends in the healing process. New Age healers are trying to accomplish what Native American healers did for thousands of years.

Today Native American healers, especially those who live in western regions of the United States, often advertise their services but make it clear they also cooperate with United States health centers. They heal both Native Americans and non–Native Americans. Likewise, health officials working in government agencies near and inside Indian reservations may consult with Native American healers before attempting to cure patients, regardless of their ailment.

In January 1970, when conventional doctors could not save a patient, Native American medicine men took over. A near-fatal injury put Richard Oakes, a well-known Mohawk leader, in a San Francisco hospital. Oakes had been hit in the head and remained in a coma for many days. His wife asked for permission to bring in traditional Indian medicine men, but the hospital refused. After much discussion, hospital administrators and doctors decided that her request was equal to calling in a clergyman, so they allowed medicine men in Oakes's room on the condition that the hospital staff be able to observe.

Mad Bear and Peter Mitten, the two medicine men who came to cure Oakes, refused to allow anyone to watch their ceremony. After long negotiations, hospital administrators decided to allow a private ceremony if the two medicine men signed a statement releasing the hospital from any potential negligence. Despite the insult, the medicine men agreed to sign because Oakes was dying as they argued.

Mad Bear released a pair of birds to fly about the patient's head, and Peter Mitten requested freshly boiled water from a nurse stationed outside the door. Richard Oakes regained consciousness and recovered soon after the ceremony.

Conventional physicians, and many others, may find it difficult to accept that Richard Oakes recovered when treated by Native American medicine men. But he, his family, and friends are most thankful that the old medicine ways got a chance to cure.

Glossary

Achomawi   ah-chew-MA-wee

A group of people who lived in northeastern California

Acoma   a-keh-mu

Native Americans who live in west central New Mexico

Algonquian   al-gon-KEE-in

The language spoken by a number of tribes, including the Arapaho, Cheyenne, Blackfoot, and Chippewa

Aztec   AZ-tek

An advanced civilization living in Mexico before Cortés's conquest in 1519

Catawba   keh-TAW-beh

Native Americans who lived along the Catawba River in the Carolinas

Cherokee   CHER-eh-kee

Southeastern tribes who lived in northern Georgia, eastern Tennessee, and western North Carolina

Chippewa   CHIP-eh-waw

A woodland tribe who lived west of the Great Lakes in Canada, Michigan, Minnesota, and Wisconsin

Comanche   ke-MAN-chee

A Great Plains tribe who lived in the Rocky Mountains of northern Texas, eastern Oklahoma, southwestern Kansas, and southwestern Colorado

Corn Husk Society

A Seneca society that participated in Midwinter events celebrated by Iroquoian-speaking tribes who lived in New York State and Canada

Creek

A southeastern tribe who lived in Alabama, Georgia, and Tennessee

Dakota   DEH-ko-teh

The largest tribe of Siouan-speaking Native Americans who lived in Minnesota and Wisconsin

False Face Society

A society of Iroquoian-speaking tribes who participated in healing ceremonies during annual Midwinter events. The tribes lived in New York State and Canada.

Fox

A tribe who lived in the area of Lake Winnebago in Wisconsin

Guardian spirit	A presence, or superego, that remained with individuals for life. Sought by many Native American groups
Haida HIGH-deh	A Northwest Coast group who lived on the Queen Charlotte Islands, British Columbia, and Prince of Wales Island, Alaska
Hopi HO-pee	Native Americans who live on three mesas in northern Arizona
Iroquoian EER-eh-kwoy-an	The language spoken by a number of Native Americans, including the Mohawk, Oneida, Onondaga, Cayuga, Seneca, Tuscarora, Huron, and Cherokee
Iroquois EER-eh-kwoy	The name commonly used to refer to the Mohawk, Oneida, Onondaga, Cayuga, Seneca, and Tuscarora, members of the Iroquois Confederacy
Karok KA-rahk	Native Americans who lived in northern California along the Klamath River
Kwakiutl KWAH-kee-oot-l	Native Americans who lived on Vancouver Island
Luiseño LOO-wi-say-nyo	Native Americans who lived along the southern California

	coast, near present-day Los Angeles
Manitou MAN-eh-toe	The cause, force, or mystical energy assumed by Algonquian-speaking tribes to be inherent in every one of nature's beings. It affects and controls the welfare of humans.
Maricopa mar-eh-KOOP-eh	Native Americans who lived along the Gila River in south central Arizona
Mayan MA-yen	Natives who lived in Yucatán, British Honduras, and northern Guatemala
Medicine bundle	A soft bag made from animal skin which holds sacred objects
Menominee men-OM-i-nee	Native Americans who lived along the Menominee River between Wisconsin and Michigan
Miami my-AM-ee	Native Americans who lived near Green Bay, Wisconsin
Micmac MIK-mak	Native Americans who lived in northern New Brunswick, on the Gaspé Peninsula of Quebec, Prince Edward Island, Cape Breton, and Nova Scotia

Midewiwin Society
       mi-deh-WEE-win   A woodland society, popular among Chippewa tribes, organized to restore and maintain tribal knowledge about herbs, myths, and legends

Montagnais   MAN-tan-yah   Native Americans who lived in Quebec and Labrador

Navajo   NAV-eh-ho   Native Americans who live in New Mexico, Arizona, and Utah

Omaha   oh-meh-HA   Native Americans who lived in northeastern Nebraska

Orenda   oh-REN-dah   *See* Manitou

Papago   PA-peh-go   Native Americans who lived in the Sonoran Desert, south of the Gila River in Arizona

Penobscot   pen-OB-scot   Native Americans who lived in Maine along the Penobscot River

Pequot   PEE-kwot   Native Americans who lived east of the Connecticut River

Pima   PEE-meh   Native Americans who lived along the Gila and Salt rivers in southern Arizona

Pipestone   A hard, reddish, claylike stone used by Native Americans to make sacred pipes

Pomo PO-mo	Native Americans who lived in northern California
Ponca PAN-keh	Native Americans who lived in northeastern Nebraska
Potawatomi PO-teh-wa-teh-me	Native Americans who lived along the eastern shores of Lake Michigan
Pueblo PWEB-low	The Spanish word for village. A general term used for all Native Americans who lived in adobe or stone villages in New Mexico and Arizona
Quechua KECH-wa	Natives of South America who lived in the former Inca Empire
Salish SAL-ish	The language spoken by many different people who lived in the Northwest. The Flathead people are often referred to as the Salish.
Sauk SAWK	Native Americans who lived in Michigan, Wisconsin, and Illinois
Seminole SEM-eh-nol	Native Americans who lived in the Florida Everglades
Shaman SHA-men	A person capable of communicating with supernatural spirits

Shasta	SHAS-ta	Native Americans who lived along the California-Oregon border
Siouan	SOO-an	The language spoken by many Native Americans, including the Mandan, Dakota, Crow, Omaha, Osage, and Hidatsa
Sioux	SOO	The name commonly used to refer to the Tetons, a band of the western Dakota
Sucking doctor		A person called to suck fluids and other harmful materials from a person's body. Many sucking doctors had supernatural powers.
Sun dance		A sacred dance performed annually by Siouan-speaking tribesmen in which men put skewers through their flesh and danced until the flesh broke. This was the most supreme offering that could possibly be made to spirits.
Tirawa	TEE-ra-wa	*See* Manitou
Tlingit	CLING-git	Native Americans who lived along the southeastern Alaska coastline
Wakan Tanka	WA-ken-tan-keh	*See* Manitou

Winnebago   win-eh-BAY-go

Native Americans who lived along the shores of Green Bay in Wisconsin

Yokut   YOO-cut

Native Americans who lived in the San Joaquin Valley and Sierra Nevada Mountains in California

Bibliography and Suggested Reading

(*Indicates titles of interest to young readers)

Aginsky, Burt W. and Ethel. *Deep Valley.* New York: Stein and Company, 1967.

Allen, Paula Gunn. *Spider Woman's Granddaughters.* Boston: Beacon Press, 1989.

Amoss, Pamela. *Coast Salish Spirit Dancing: The Survival of an Ancestral Religion.* Seattle: University of Washington Press, 1978.

Barbeau, Marius. *Medicine-Men of the North Pacific Coast. Department of Northern Affairs and National Resources Bulletin,* no. 152, Anthropological Series no. 42: National Museum of Canada, 1958.

Bear, Luther Standing. *Land of the Spotted Eagle.* Lincoln, Nebraska: University of Nebraska Press, 1978.

Beauchamp, William. *The Iroquois or Footprints of the Six Nations.* Fayetteville, New York: Beauchamp Recorder Office, 1892.

*Beck, Horace P. *Gluskap the Liar and Other Indian Tales.* Freeport, Maine: Bond Wheelwright Company, 1966.

*Beck, Peggy V., and Anna L. Walters. *The Sacred: Ways of Knowledge, Sources of Life.* Tsaile (Navajo Nation), Arizona: Navajo Community College Press, 1977.

Benedict, Ruth Fulton. "The Concept of the Guardian Spirit in North

America," *Memoirs of the American Anthropological Association,* no. 29. Menasha, Wisconsin: Collegiate Press, 1923.

*Bierhorst, John, ed. *Four Masterpieces of American Indian Literature.* Tucson: University of Arizona Press, 1974.

*———. *The Mythology of North America.* New York: William Morrow, 1985.

Boyd, Doug. *Rolling Thunder.* New York: Dell, 1974.

Brass, Eleanor. *Medicine Boy and Other Cree Tales.* Calgary, Canada. Glenbow-Alberta Institute, 1979.

Brinton, Daniel G., M.D. *Myths of the Americas: The Symbolism and Mythology of the Indians of the Americas.* New York: Rudolf Steiner Publications, 1976.

Brotherston, Gordon. *Image of the New World: The American Continent Portrayed in Native Texts.* London: Thames and Hudson, 1979.

Brown, Dorothy Moulding. *Indian Tree Myths and Legends.* Wisconsin Archeologist, vol. 19, no. 2. Milwaukee: New Series, 1938.

Brown, Joseph Epes. *The Spiritual Legacy of the American Indian.* New York: Crossroad Publishing Company, 1987.

Brown, Michael Fobes. "Dark Side of the Shaman." *Natural History* (November 1989), 8–10.

*Caduto, Michael J., and Joseph Bruchac. *Keepers of the Earth: Native American Stories and Environmental Activities for Children.* Golden, Colorado: Fulcrum, 1988.

Campbell, Joseph. *Historical Atlas of World Mythology.* Vol. I, *The Way of the Animal Powers.* Pt. 2, "Mythologies of the Great Hunt." New York: Harper and Row, 1988.

———. *Historical Atlas of World Mythology.* Vol. II, *The Way of the Seeded Earth.* Pt. 1, "The Sacrifice." New York: Harper and Row, 1988.

———. *Primitive Mythology: The Masks of God.* New York: Penguin Books, 1976.

*Carter, Forrest. *The Education of Little Tree.* Albuquerque: University of New Mexico Press, 1976.

Carter, W. H., and G. B. Fenstermaker. *Seneca Indians: Guardians of the Western Door of the League of the Iroquois Longhouse — The Home, Life and Culture.* London, Ontario: North American Indian Publications, 1974.

*Clark, Ella E. *Indian Legends from the Northern Rockies.* Norman: University of Oklahoma Press, 1966.

Castaneda, Carlos. *The Teachings of Don Juan: A Yaqui Way of Knowledge.* New York: Pocket Books, 1968.

Corlett, William Thomas, M.D. *The Medicine-Man of the American Indian and His Cultural Background.* Springfield, Illinois: Charles C. Thomas, 1935.

*D'Azevedo, Warren L., ed. *Handbook of North American Indians,* vol. 11, Great Basin. Washington, D.C.: Smithsonian Institution, 1986.

Deloria, Vine, Jr. *God is Red.* New York: Dell, 1973.

———. *The Metaphysics of Modern Existence.* New York: Harper and Row, 1979.

DeMallie, Raymond J., and Douglas R. Parks, eds. *Sioux Indian Religion.* Norman: University of Oklahoma Press, 1987.

*Densmore, Frances. *How Indians Use Wild Plants for Food, Medicine and Crafts.* New York: Dover Publications, 1974.

*deWit, Dorothy, ed. *The Talking Stone: An Anthology of Native American Tales and Legends.* New York: Greenwillow Books, 1979.

Diamond, Stanley, ed. *Primitive Views of the World.* New York: Columbia University Press, 1964.

Driver, Harold E. *Indians of North America.* Chicago: University of Chicago Press, 1961.

Elsmore, Frances. "The Shaman and Modern Medicines." *El Palacio* XLII, nos. 45–46 (January 27–February 10, 1937).

*Erdoes, Richard, and Alfonso Ortiz, eds. *American Indian Myths and Legends.* New York: Pantheon Books, 1984.

Evers, Larry, ed. *Between Sacred Mountains: Navajo Stories and Lessons from the Land.* Tucson: Sun Tracks and the University of Arizona Press, 1982.

Fagan, Brian M. *Clash of Cultures.* New York: W. H. Freeman and Company, 1984.

Garbarino, Merwyn S. *Native American Heritage.* Boston: Little, Brown and Company, 1976.

Grieve, Mrs. M. *A Modern Herbal.* 2 vols. New York: Dover Publications, 1971.

Grinnell, George Bird. *Pawnee, Blackfoot and Cheyenne: History and Folklore of the Plains.* New York: Charles Scribner's Sons, 1961.

Harner, Michael. *The Way of the Shaman.* New York: Bantam Books, 1982.

Hausman, Gerald, ed. *Meditations with Animals: A Native American Bestiary.* Sante Fe: Bear & Company, 1986.

Hedrick, U. P., ed. *Sturtevant's Edible Plants of the World.* New York: Dover Publications, 1972.

*Heizer, Robert F., ed. *Handbook of North American Indians,* Vol. 8, California. Washington, D.C.: Smithsonian Institution, 1978.

Henry, Jeannette, and Rupert Costo. *A Thousand Years of American Indian Storytelling.* San Francisco: Indian Historian Press, 1981.

Hultkrantz, Ake. *Belief and Worship in Native North America.* Syracuse, New York: Syracuse University Press, 1981.

———. *Native Religions of North America.* San Francisco: Harper and Row, 1987.

*Kavasch, Barrie. *Native Harvests.* New York: Vintage Books, 1979.

Kluckhohn, Clyde. *Navaho Witchcraft.* Boston: Beacon Press, 1944.

*Kroeber, A. L. *Handbook of the Indians of California.* New York: Dover Publications, 1976.

Kutenai, Kachinas, R.N., M.D. *Medicine Woman Speaks.* Sparks, Nevada: Kutenai's Respect All Culture Publishers, Inc. 1981.

*Lame Deer, John (Fire), and Richard Erdoes. *Lame Deer: Seeker of Visions.* New York: Washington Square Press, 1972.

Lévi-Strauss, Claude. *The Origin of Table Manners.* New York: Harper and Row, 1979.

Luckert, Karl W. *Coyoteway: A Navajo Holyway Healing Ceremonial.* Tucson: The University of Arizona Press, and Flagstaff: Museum of Northern Arizona Press, 1979.

McGaa, Ed (Eagle Man). *Mother Earth: Native American Paths to Healing Ourselves and Our World.* San Francisco: HarperCollins Publishers, 1990.

Malinowski, Bronislaw. *Magic, Science and Religion and Other Essays.* Garden City, New York: Doubleday and Company, 1954.

*Marriott, Alice, and Carol K. Rachlin. *American Indian Mythology.* New York: Thomas Y. Crowell Company, 1968.

Maslow, Abraham H. *Toward a Psychology of Being.* New York: Van Nostrand Reinhold, 1968.

*Moerman, Daniel E. *Geraniums for the Iroquois: A Field Guide to American Indian Medicinal Plants.* Algonac, Michigan: Reference Publications, 1982.

Mooney, James. "Cherokee Theory and Practice of Medicine." *Journal of American Folk-Lore* (1890): 44–50.

Morgan, L. H. *League of the Ho-de-no-sau-nee or Iroquois.* New Haven: Yale University Press, 1954.

*Neihardt, John G. *Black Elk Speaks.* Lincoln: University of Nebraska Press, 1961.

Nequatewa, Edmond. *Truth of a Hopi and Other Clan Stories of Shung-Opovi.* Edited by Mary-Russell F. Colton. *Museum of Northern Arizona Bulletin,* no. 8. Flagstaff: Northern Arizona Society of Science and Art, 1936.

*Ortiz, Alfonso, ed. *Handbook of North American Indians,* vols. 9 and 10, Southwest. Washington, D.C.: Smithsonian Institution, 1979 and 1983.

——. *The Tewa World.* Chicago: University of Chicago Press, 1969.

*Palmer, Lawrence E. *Fieldbook of Natural History.* New York: McGraw Hill, 1975.

Parker, Arthur C. "Indian Medicine and Medicine Men," *36th Annual Archaeological Report.* Toronto: Ontario Provincial Museum, 1928.

Parsons, Elsie Clews, ed. *American Indian Life.* Lincoln: University of Nebraska Press, 1922.

*Peattie, Donald Culross. *A Natural History of Trees of Eastern and Central North America.* New York: Bonanza Books, 1948.

Powers, Marla N. *Oglala Women: Myth, Ritual, and Reality.* Chicago: University of Chicago Press, 1986.

*Radin, Paul. *The Autobiography of a Winnebago Indian.* New York: Dover Publications, 1963.

River, W. H. R. *Medicine, Magic, and Religion.* New York: Harcourt, Brace & Company, 1924.

Schlesier, Karl H. *The Wolves of Heaven: Cheyenne Shamanism, Ceremonies, and Prehistoric Origins.* Norman: University of Oklahoma Press, 1987.

Schoolcraft, Henry Rowe. *Historical and Statistical Information Respecting the History and Prospects of the Indian Tribes of the United States.* 6 vols. Philadelphia: J. P. Lippincott, 1851–57.

Silko, Leslie Marmon. *Ceremony.* New York: New American Library, 1977.

*Spence, Lewis. *North American Indians: Myths and Legends.* New York: Avenal Books, 1985.

Spencer, Robert F., et al. *The Native Americans.* New York: Harper and Row, 1977.

Spindler, George, and Louise Spindler. *Dreamers with Power: The Menominee.* Prospect Heights, Illinois: Waveland Press, 1971.

Steiger, Brad. *Medicine Power: The American Indian's Revival of His*

Spiritual Heritage and Its Relevance for Modern Man. New York: Doubleday and Company, 1974.

Steinmetz, Paul B. *Meditations with Native Americans — Lakota Spirituality.* Santa Fe, New Mexico: Bear and Company, 1984.

Stone, Eric P., M.D. *Medicine Among the American Indians.* New York: Paul B. Hoeber, 1932.

Storm, Hyemeyohsts. *Seven Arrows.* New York: Ballantine Books, 1972.

———. *Song of Heyoehkah.* San Francisco: Harper and Row, 1981.

Swanton, John R. *The Indians of the Southeastern United States.* Washington, D.C.: Smithsonian Institution, 1946.

*Tantaquidgeon, Gladys. *Folk Medicine of the Delaware and Related Algonkian Indians.* Harrisburg: Pennsylvania Historical and Museum Commission, 1977.

Tedlock, Dennis, and Barbara Tedlock, eds. *Teachings from the American Earth: Indian Religion and Philosophy.* New York: Liveright, 1975.

Tooker, Elisabeth. *The Iroquois Ceremonial of Midwinter.* Syracuse: Syracuse University Press, 1970.

*———. *An Iroquois Source Book,* vol. 3, Medicine Society Rituals. New York: Garland Publishing, 1986.

———, ed. *Native North American Spirituality of the Eastern Wood-lands.* Mahwah, New Jersey: Paulist Press, 1979.

*Trigger, Bruce G., ed. *Handbook of North American Indians,* vol. 15, Northeast. Washington, D.C.: Smithsonian Institution, 1978.

*Turner, Frederick W. III, ed. *The Portable North American Indian Reader.* New York: Viking Press, 1973.

Underhill, Ruth M. *Red Man's America.* Chicago: University of Chicago Press, 1953.

———. *Red Man's Religion: Beliefs and Practices of the Indians North of Mexico.* Chicago: University of Chicago Press, 1965.

Vecsey, Christopher, and Robert W. Venables, eds. *American Indian Environments: Ecological Issues in Native American History.* Syracuse: Syracuse University Press, 1980.

*Vogel, Virgil J. *American Indian Medicine.* Norman: University of Oklahoma Press, 1970.

Waugh, Earle H., and K. Dad Prithipaul, eds. *Native Religious Traditions. Canadian Corporation of Studies in Religion Supplement,* no. 8. Waterloo, Ontario: Wilfrid Laurier University Press, 1977.

Waters, Frank. *Book of the Hopi.* New York: Penguin Books, 1977.

*Weatherford, Jack. *Indian Givers: How the Indians of the Americas Transformed the World.* New York: Crown Publishers, 1988.

*Weiner, Michael. *Earth Medicine, Earth Food.* New York: Macmillan Publishing Company, 1972.

*Witt, Shirley Hill, and Stan Steiner, eds. *The Way: An Anthology of American Indian Literature.* New York: Alfred A. Knopf, 1972.

Wissler, Clark. "The Functions of Primitive Ritualistic Ceremonies," *Popular Science Monthly,* August 1915, 200–203.

———. "The Indian and the Supernatural." *Natural History,* vol. XLII, June–December 1938, 121–126, 154.

*Wood, Marion. *Spirits, Heroes and Hunters from North American Indian Mythology.* New York: Schocken Books, 1982.

*Zitkala-Sa. *Old Indian Legends.* Lincoln: University of Nebraska Press, 1985.

Index